SEMS REDUX

Set your Goals
&
Seek your Dreams

Charles Wahr

CHARLES TICHY

SEMS REDUX

TATE PUBLISHING
AND ENTERPRISES, LLC

Published by Tate Publishing & Enterprises, LLC
127 E. Trade Center Terrace | Mustang, Oklahoma 73064 USA
1.888.361.9473 | www.tatepublishing.com

Tate Publishing is committed to excellence in the publishing industry. The company reflects the philosophy established by the founders, based on Psalm 68:11,
"The Lord gave the word and great was the company of those who published it."

Book design copyright © 2012 by Tate Publishing, LLC. All rights reserved.
Cover design by Kristen Verser
Interior design by April Marciszewski
Photographs by Paulissa Kipp
Locker room and equipment provided by Tyler Zahn, Ralston High School head football coach

Published in the United States of America

ISBN: 978-1-61862-737-7
1. Fiction / Sports
2. Fiction / Biographical
12.05.18

DEDICATION

I would like to dedicate this story to my lovely wife, Karen; the adjunct faculty at Metropolitan Community College; and the doctors and nurses at the VA who have put up with me during the time it took this project to be completed.

Sems Redux is a story based on the writer's experiences and dream. It is dedicated to those in our society who are over the age of fifty, especially those well over fifty. Some names have been changed to protect those who still consider themselves innocent.

CHAPTER 1

I t is a typical late November evening in the Midwest—
Omaha, Nebraska, to be exact. More specifically, it's
Friday night at Omaha Metro Stadium, the home of
the new, and quite successful, Omaha Bulldog professional football team. In the "old days," this team would
have been called "semi-professional," because it is one
step below the ranks of the National Football League.
Being in Nebraska, where football is a major part of
most people's lives, the Bulldogs, as predicted, is a team
that has had an unusually strong following for its initial season. The question is why? That's what this story
is about. Now, let's go to Bulldog Stadium where we
will check out the closing minutes of the Professional
Football Conference championship game.

As we make our way through downtown Omaha,
we will catch a glimpse of just about every bar, pub,
or tavern that has a large flat screen TV, and see the

multitudes of fans cheering their Bulldogs on! As we get to the stadium, we quickly learn that there are no parking spaces left, and as usual, no seats left either. As predicted, this game is sold out. Besides, it's the conference championship game! The only thing left to do is tune into the local radio station and find out what's going on.

"This is Stu Lerner, your announcer for the Bulldogs at Omaha Metro Stadium. I'm here with Fred Reeger, former all-star NFL quarterback, who's helping me commentate on this outstanding professional conference championship game between the Sacramento Sun Devils and last season's champs, the Omaha Bulldogs. It's late in the fourth quarter with the home Dogs ahead of the Tampa Bay Vampires by a touchdown. Fred, are you thinking what I'm thinking?"

"I don't believe it, Stu. Are you kidding me? I wouldn't have believed it, if I hadn't seen it myself! Wow! That was JT's second TD of the evening. So far, it has been pretty close, Stu. After getting the ball back with less than two minutes to play, all the Dogs have to do is keep possession of the ball and keep it on the ground with long counts as they've done in the first two downs. Okay, it's third down coming up. This crowd is going nuts, back to you, Stu!"

"This is Stu Lerner with Fred Reeger from Bulldog Stadium in Omaha, Nebraska. It's third down, and the Dogs break their huddle. It's the 'I' formation with Jones at wide out, left. Quarterback Lefebvre lines up to take the snap, halfback Morris behind Lefebvre, and JT at deep back. The ball is snapped after a long count, Lefebvre fakes it to Morris, who charges through the Vampire D-line. Lefebvre steps back, looks, and fakes a pass to his wide out, then gives the ball to JT, who shoots off tackle. He breaks through the line, peels away from a defender, and darts into the Viper secondary, sidestepping his way!"

"Oh Stu! Oh Stu! I can't believe it! He's broken loose again! Look at him go! Look at him go! Are you kidding me? Are you kidding me?

"JT is running free and untouched again, past the fifty yard line and across the Vampire forty... the thirty..."

"Stu! Stu! He's going all the way! How does he do it? How does he do it?"

"JT is in the end zone for his third TD of the evening, with less than a minute left, this should ice it for the Dogs! The crowd is going berserk again and chanting, 'JT! JT! JT!' We'll turn up the volume so you can hear it!"

Sure enough, the Omaha Bulldogs win the conference championship game thanks to JT and his outstanding play. But why him? What makes him so spectacular, even in the eyes of that former all-star NFL quarterback, Fred Reeger, who proclaimed JT as "one of the most spectacular football players in the history of professional football!" But the question is why him? Why are we questioning JT's performance in particular? Couldn't he have had just an outstanding season as any other running back, or any other football player? What makes JT so special? And one more burning question: why haven't any of the National Football League franchises scooped this "phenom" up by now?

CHAPTER 2

Well, in order to learn the answers to these questions, and the "wonder" of JT, we must initially go back to December of 1974. No, that is definitely not the date of JT's birth! If your math is decent you'll soon learn, or if you haven't figured it out already, some answers to all this astonishment.

The place is not the typical press box of any football stadium, and it doesn't matter that the weather on this late evening is rather dreary, foggy, and wet. These conditions only enhance the sight of this sacred athletic venue. As the stadium lights shine through the haze, one can see the elegant Romanesque columns with its arches, casting the prestigious, breathtaking image of Soldier Field in Chicago, Illinois. A radio announcer, sitting behind his microphone, excitedly says, "Wow! What a quality championship football game! Here we are, up in the press box at the grand and famous Soldier Field in Chicago. I'm so proud to have been a part of this event, football fans! The semi-professional football champions, the Long Island Chiefs have just beat the San Diego Spartans in one of the best gridiron contests that I've seen, even in the pros. I'm Dick Turner, and I've been here at Soldier Field announcing with Fred Russell on your local sports radio station, KWBIS. Fred is now down on the field with one of the stars of the game, Long Island Chiefs' JT Tichi. JT—and as you already know, or if you just tuned in—not only excelled as the Chiefs' wide receiver, with four receptions and a TD, but he also made two interceptions on the other side of the ball at cornerback, and returned one of those for a touchdown late in the game. Take it away, Fred."

Down on the football field, announcer Fred Russell, with a microphone in hand and squeezing his way amongst exuberant fans, reports. "Okay, Dick. I'm here on the field with the star of this championship game, JT Tichi, and his celebrating teammates. JT—how does it feel being the champs of the American Semi-Professional Football League?"

"Just great, Dick. I'm so very proud to be a member of this team. We worked vey hard to get here."

Dick, pushed a bit by the other celebrants asks, "How were you able to go both ways… and even score on both sides of the ball? This would be unheard of in the pros. "

Smiling, JT joyfully replies, "I have only my team-mates and this great coaching staff to thank. Without them and their talents, we just wouldn't be here, Dick, and I certainly would not have had those opportunities. And you're right, Dick, this ain't the pros!"

"Speaking of the pros, JT, would I be out of line saying that this performance, and this whole season for that matter, raises your chances of our seeing you in Kansas City next year?"

JT laughs and answers, "As you know, Dick, I'm a high school teacher, and I'm really beginning to love it, and…"

"But the pros, JT…the pros," interrupts the sports-caster. "Wouldn't that be a bit more lucrative for you?"

"For me, it would be a difficult descision, Dick. It's hard to say, Dick. We'll just see. We'll just see."

Now let's advance in time to the following spring, 1975. It's a late afternoon in early April, at the men's locker room at West Babylon High School in Long Island, New York. This is the practice facility of the Long Island Chiefs, the affiliate of the professional football team, the Kansas City Chiefs. It's the first day of spring practice for the team, and there is supposed to be a team meeting. In walks Joe Tichi, that's Joseph Gerald Tichi. The last name pronounced as if the "c" is an "s." To lessen any confusion with mispronunciation of his last name, Joe accepted the shortened version to just "JT." This started in high school and throughout his four-year stint in the military, and for nine years as an electric utility lineman. Upon the chalkboard is a notice: JT—report to the coaches' office ASAP.

JT makes his way to the coaches' office and knocks. A voice from behind the door shouts, "Enter!"

JT walks in to find the head coach, Marcus Anderson; running backs' coach Dan Mosemann; and a primary owner of the Long Island Chiefs' franchise, Elmer Dugan.

Head coach Anderson opens the conversation. "JT…ah…we've asked you to…ah… come in to…um talk…or um…

"We've got to talk about and consider your future," interrupted club owner Dugan.

"Yeah, JT… it's about…your um, ah… your…" stammers Anderson.

"Okay, okay! Look, JT." pipes in running backs' coach Mosemann. "We've got to give this to you straight."

"Please do," interjects JT. "But I kind of know where you all are trying to go with this. Just relax and tell me exactly what it is."

Anderson takes a deep breath and continues, "Now look. You've done quite well for our initial three seasons. But the main reason why the pros won't… ah, you know, call you up is… ah… because of… ah."

Mosemann gestures with his hand, "Because, ah... you're, ah...

Dugan is just about to finish his sentence, when JT ends it for them. "Too danged old!"

"Yes! Yes! You're thirty five years old!" Dugan chimes in. One could almost hear the deep sighs of relief from the coaches.

"We, the owners and I, are prepared to cut a small kind of severance deal for you," continued Dugan with a smile. "That's because you really did such a fine job in helping to establish this franchise. But you've got to..."

Before Dugan can finish his sentence—and to the coaches', and his own, obvious astonishment—the three notice a warm smile appearing on JT's face.

"You've got to understand," Anderson interjects, "the whole medical aspect."

"Yes," Dugan continues, "you should know that medical science says that the older you become, the more one is susceptible to broken bones, arterial problems, lung, joints, ligaments..."

"Yes, yes, I know all that," JT replies with that smile still on his face. "It's just that, well, ah, by coincidence, I was actually trying to find a way to explain to you why I needed to take some time off anyway! Look, I love playing this game, but to be honest, I have a lot on my plate right now. You know, obligations at home, and I just began teaching. I'm also planning to begin a post-graduate program at NYU. I just learned that I've been accepted for a study abroad doctoral program, and it begins in June. I'll be going to London and West Breton Hall College of Education in England. I'm supposed to leave a week after the last day of school in June."

The owner and coaches have a satisfied look of relief and amazement on their faces while JT continues. "And by all means, I'll kindly accept that severance deal. The kids are growing fast, and we sure could use the extra bucks. Thank you! Thank you all."

He extends his hand, smiles, and shakes hands with the coaches and owner. Anderson gives him a bear hug and says, "We're going to miss you, JT."

Mosemann follows with his handshake and a bear hug, and adds, "When you get to Merry Old England, say 'hi' to the Queen for me!"

CHAPTER 3

After his stint studying abroad, JT continued to teach at the high school in New York. While continuing his post-graduate studies at NYU, he also accepted the position of an assistant football coach at the high school. If that wasn't enough to keep him busy, he also became the speech and debate team coach! These anomalous duties only seemed to make JT an excellent role model for many of his students.

As the years rolled by, JT missed playing football more and more. As an assistant football coach, the team, as well as the coaching staff, were always astonished by JT's athleticism. Not only would he participate in the calisthenics, he always seemed to be amongst the leaders in the wind sprints. During his early coaching experiences, JT could not understand why his running backs just were not as agile as he was, especially when it came time to pivot and make fakes.

He soon learned to deliver the adage, "If I can do it, so can you!"

By 1980, his post-graduate class work was winding down; however, the topic for his doctoral dissertation would require his relocation from New York to Omaha, Nebraska. Finding employment in Omaha was not a problem for JT. Because of his diversified educational background, he had his pick of employment as a secondary English, speech and/or debate teacher. He was also available to coach football and be the speech and debate adviser. Still, JT missed playing football.

Nevertheless, in 1981, he accepted a high school position where he taught English, public speaking, and debate. He also accepted the extra duty positions of assistant football coach and debate coach. JT remained diligent in completing his research. By 1988, he received his doctoral degree from NYU.

JT remained teaching and coaching at the high school. Still missing playing football, he soon decided to teach part time on the college level. It was at this academic level where he discovered that his pedagogic experiences were enjoyed the most. With a desire to teach more classes at the local community college and university, JT retired from the high school in 2002 and took on more college classes. Since this move took him out of coaching high school football, he now missed playing football more than ever.

CHAPTER 4

It's now the spring of 2010, and JT is approaching his seventieth birthday. He is still an adjunct at the local community college, teaching as many classes as he is allowed. As usual, the local news media—newspaper, television, and radio— is covering the spring football practices for the University of Nebraska football team. The hype is alive and well—Go Big Red! JT still misses the game.

It's a pleasant, early April morning. JT is in his living room completing his daily regimen of seventy-five sit-ups (crunches) followed by seventy-five push-ups. This is the same exercise routine that JT has maintained since his Marine Corps boot camp days at Paris Island. Kay, JT's wife and a high school counselor, appears from the kitchen. She is decked out in a bright apron and waving a spatula in one hand as she asks, "How many eggs and pancakes would you like this morning? You know I have to keep you healthy!"

"Two and three." JT mumbles as he finishes his push-ups.

Kay disappears back into the kitchen, and JT finishes his exercises by stretching and finally sits down on his favorite chair, and begins reading the newspaper. Then with a sudden jolt, he springs up from his sitting position and blurts out a sigh, then gasps, and shouts, "Oh my God! I don't believe it! Kay! Kay! Come here! Did you read this? Kay! Kay!"

Kay reappears from the kitchen with a shocked expression with a mixing spoon in her hand. She nervously inquires, "What? What? What on earth is wrong?"

"Would you believe they're thinking of having a professional football franchise right here in Omaha?" JT answers. "Wow! How about that? I mean, right here in Omaha!"

With a look of utter disbelief, and obviously relieved, Kay replies, "Like, so what? Here, I thought you were having some kind of stroke or something, and it's just about a lousy football team! Geez!"

"But, honey! They're going to call them the Bull Dogs, and…" JT retorts.

Shaking her head in disbelief, Kay shrugs with a, "Humph!"

JT continues excitedly, "Look, they've even begun scheduling try-outs! And, and they're expecting to see some old NFL-ers! Wow!"

"So? Like, so what?" Kay retorts.

"You don't suppose that…" JT looks up mournfully.

"Now you're not…No, you're not thinking of… don't be silly! Well, coaching, maybe…but not… No!" Kay tries to interject.

"Well um, I could try. Like, ah, I wouldn't mind trying…" JT ends with a mumble, looking mournfully, and peeking up at her.

Kay, with one hand on her hip and with the other pointing her mixing spoon at JT for emphasis. "Joseph Gerald Tichi! Are you out of your freaking mind? No! No! No!" This ends the conversation. Kay lowers her mixing spoon and retreats back into her kitchen with a final, "Humph!"

Later that same day, JT experiences an ironic situation with one of his community college students. At the end of his argumentation and debate class, while his students are exiting, one of them, Brad Smithson, approaches the lectern.

He patiently waits for another student to end a brief conversation with JT. Then Brad reports, "Dr. Tichi, it looks like I might have to miss a couple classes next month, I have a conflict."

Grasping this "teaching moment," JT inquires, "Might? Will you or won't you? And what may I ask is this 'conflict,' Brad?"

"Well, um… I…um…I'm pretty sure that I'll be trying out for the…um, that new pro football team that's going to be here in town." Brad replies.

JT continues his teaching moment, "Do you mean the Omaha Bull Dogs?"

"Yes." Brad slowly nods.

"Reading comprehension!" JT retorts. "Mind your reading comprehension, son! According to *The Herald*, those tryouts are being scheduled for six in the evening, during the weekdays, and all day on Saturdays at the old baseball stadium down town. I really don't foresee any conflict, since this class meets at noon and ends at two!"

"Oh! Wow! You read the article too?" Brad asks with a smile. "I'm sorry. I kind of missed those scheduling times. So, I guess I won't be missing any of your classes after all!"

Lowering his voice, JT replies, "You know, Brad, you have to really improve your reading comp skills. It's going to give you some serious problems down the road, not only in this class, but especially in others. The evidence and proof you'll be citing will have to be right on!"

"Yes sir." Brad answers. "I'm going to work on it."

"Okay." JT changes the subject. "What position will you be trying out for?"

"D-back, um…Cornerback, or safety." Brad answers and opens up. "I was all-state back in high school, a few years back. But I screwed up a scholarship at Iowa State, and here I am, working on an associate's degree so that I can eventually transfer into the university."

"And you're going to give the sems a shot."

"Sems? Sems, what's that?" asks Brad.

"Well, back in the old days, when…" JT answers, as they both begin to exit the classroom.

They proceed out of the building and into the parking lot. JT continues, "And do you remember Mickey Rupert, you know that old quarterback from the Packers, and Shane Parks, that running back from the Bears?"

"Yeah, they're supposed to be trying out too!" Brad answers.

JT continues, "Holy cow! And what about…."

CHAPTER 5

After a somewhat quiet dinner that evening, JT and Kay are cleaning the dishes from the table, and going back and forth to the dishwasher.

JT begins, "Kay, we need to sit down and talk."

"Uh oh! What did I do this time? Or, No! What did *you* do this time?" quips Kay, as they find their way into the living room and sit down.

JT begins again. "Well, after a conversation with one of my students, who, coincidentally, is going to try out for that new Omaha football team, I am seriously considering …"

"Just stop right there, Joe!" Kay interrupts. "You have to really stop, think, and realize exactly what you're thinking of doing."

"Yes, Kay, I have, and…" JT tries to explain.

"What? Are you out of your mind? Are you completely nuts?" Kay rants. "You're smarter than this. You're an educated person! You have graduate degrees!"

"But I know that… " JT attempts again.

"Don't you realize that you can severely hurt yourself?" Kay screams. "Don't you realize that if you don't incapacitate yourself doing this at your age, you could possibly kill yourself?"

"Yes, but let me just…" JT sadly tries to interject.

"Oh, Joe, Joey, you know that I love you so much, and I want you around forever, and as healthy as ever." Kay finally stops and sobs.

JT slowly takes advantage of this respite and begins, "Please, Kay. I… I love you so much too, but let me explain."

While Kay continues to sob quietly, JT continues. "Look, sweetheart, it's just that I have this, and have had this, urge, and maddening desire to finish something I love and have loved all my life. I just see this as that opportunity. Sure, it sounds silly."

Kay looks up and just slowly shakes her head, still in disbelief.

"If I can't, there will be an aching space inside me that will stay with me, there forever."

JT slowly rises and reaches over to Kay with both hands. He guides her to stand up and continues, gazing into each other's eyes. "But I do know this. I've always known my body, and I've always known my limits. And I promise you that I will quit when my health is in peril." They embrace.

After the long hug, Kay breaks away and says with a smirk, "Okay! Okay! You dumb jerk! No, jerk isn't good enough for you. What was it in high school? Oh, yes, I remember! It was dork! Okay, you big dork! Go ahead and play your heart out!"

JT smiles and replies, "I'm okay with dork, if you're okay with ding, like in ding-dong!" They both laugh and embrace again.

"Oh, and one other thing," JT continues, "I'd like to keep this quiet for as long as we can."

Kay leaves for the kitchen. "Okay, I'm going to brew some tea." She then hesitates and asks, "But doesn't that student of yours know of your intentions?"

"Heck, no! I don't want it going all over the school that this old fart is going to do such a dumb thing!" JT laughingly replies.

Calling from the kitchen, Kay giggles back, "Oh, by the way, Sweetie, make sure that your insurance is all paid up and up-to-date!"

The next day, Friday, JT is on the telephone, inquiring about the procedure for trying out for the Bull Dogs. "Okay, I'll be right down to fill out the application."

Then he shouts, "Kay! Kay! Should I color my hair or put something on my face to hide the wrinkles or something?"

"No comment!" Kay stiffly replies.

About an hour later, a line is seen entering the old baseball stadium in downtown Omaha. JT, in sweats with a woolen cap and a hood over his head, is in the line. As he accepts the application, he is given instructions to fill it out at the nearby tables. After it's submitted, he will be notified as soon as possible.

JT takes the application, finds a table, sits down, and begins to fill out the information. Besides the name, address, birth date, and telephone number, there was a large space for previous playing experiences and positions. When he came to the place where the date of birth was asked, he paused, shrugged, and put down 11/06/39. He then proceeds to fill in nearly the whole space allowed for "experience."

After a harrowing weekend, with JT somewhat coming to the resolution that there would be no way that he will be given the chance to try out, he moans to Kay, "Once they see my date of birth, forget about it!"

Kay appears somewhat satisfied, but remains quiet.

CHAPTER 6

I n that Tuesday, JT comes home from the college to see the message light flashing on the telephone's answering machine. He reaches over and presses the message button.

"Tuesday, 9:22 a.m."

"Hi, Mimi! It's just me. I just wanted to see how you and Grandpa are doing! I love you!"

"Tuesday, 10:06 a.m."

"This is American Mutual calling about your medicare coverage, please call us at 402-399-9990 to hear about our excellent program for retirees. You'll be so pleased."

"Tuesday, 11:40 a.m."

"This is for a JT Tichi? This is Marv Stanton, the Offensive Coach for the Omaha Bulldogs. Please call me at 662-4777."

"End of messages."

Nervously, JT plays the last message over again and writes down the number. He pauses, then picks up the receiver, and dials the number.

"Stanton here, who's this?" The voice asks.

"This is JT Tichi returning your call." JT replies.

"Oh, yeah, we looked over your application, and you have some experience playing for that Long Island squad for the Chiefs." Stanton begins.

" Yeah, but... ah," JT tries to reply.

"We'll be looking for around a half dozen rb's. So far we've made the first cut on paper! We've narrowed it down to about a dozen. You should be happy about that. Now, we'll be glad to take a real look at you." The coach laughs.

"Okay, but…" JT stammers.

"So, come on down this Thursday night, at six, at the same place where you filled out the application. We'll issue you some gear and a schedule. Then, be ready to rock for a full tryout first thing, nine Saturday morning, on June 19. Be there by eight, and we'll assign you a locker. That's some five weeks from now. Will you be up for it?" The coach finishes, seemingly, all in one breath.

"Um ah, well, sure!" JT blurts out.

"Good! If you have any questions, just call. You've got my number. See you then." Stanton states.

"Ah, okay, coach. See you Thursday." JT hangs up.

He then jumps up and let's out a war whoop just as Kay comes in the front door, noticing one of JT's victory dances.

"Okay. Don't tell me—let me guess—they must have overlooked your birth date!" She declares with a smirk.

"And I don't give a big rat's butt!" JT whoops continuously. Then, he stops abruptly, and says, "Uh oh, I think I'm going to have to figure out a serious workout schedule. I only have about a month to prepare!"

That evening, JT is sitting and mumbling in front of his computer.

"Okay, let's see, a two-mile jog in the morning, push-ups and crunches, break, then some wind sprints. Then I go to class, then lunch. Then I have another class. Then I come home, lift the weights, and loosen up, then, some more wind sprints. I'll increase the morning jogs as the time goes on."

Kay comes up behind him, leans over, and says, "Please don't be mad at me, but I went ahead and made an appointment with Jen Harrington so you can get a full physical exam."

JT turns with a glare, but continues to listen.

"Now don't get mad. I just want some professional reassurance. It's for Thursday at eleven. You have to get there at ten so they can take some blood and you can leave a specimen. Oh, JT, I'm just very concerned, and after all, you are a grandfather, for goodness sakes!" Kay finishes.

"Okay, okay!" JT relents stubbornly. "You know I'm still going to try outs anyway, regardless of what Jen says!"

"Let's just listen to what she says, that's all." Kay replies.

"Okay." JT gives in. They hug.

That Thursday, JT and Kay are waiting patiently in the office of Dr. Jennifer Harrington, family physician. The doctor enters, smiles, and shakes hands with Kay and JT.

Jen gets right to the point, looks JT in the eyes, and asks, "What's this about you playing football? I mean, pro football? Are you serious?"

"You're damned right I am! Unless you have any strong objections…" JT replies with a smile.

"Okay. I see that you are serious, so I'll tell you exactly what's at stake for you, and you make your own decision," Jen replies, glancing at Kay, who remains quiet, but a bit anxious.

Jen continues. "First, your vitals are excellent. Your blood pressure and specimen breakdown numbers are all quite good for a man your age, and I must emphasize for a man your age. Secondly, if your intentions are to, um, play football," Jen pauses, "then, as you must already know, you'll be participating in a full contact activity with men twenty, or thirty, uh, less than half your, uh, more than forty years younger than you."

"So?" JT asks, with a slightly perplexed look.

"Oh, JT!" Jen explains, remaining as professional as possible. "You should know that a man at your age physiologically does not have the same make up as one who is younger, especially compared to those you're going to physically encounter. From your bone density to the flexibility of your joints and ligaments..."

"Okay, okay, Jen, I fully understand, and I fully appreciate your concern, but both you and Kay—honey, both of you—must understand my maddening desire to play once more. Yes, I fully understand the health risks. But, please understand that it's me, not you, nor anyone else. And yes, I am willing to take not only full responsibility of my limits, but I promise that I will know when to quit."

Jen looks at Kay, who is already looking at Jen.

"Yeah, you're right, Kay." Jen relents. "He is a dork!"

They both shrug, and then miraculously say in unison, "Okay, but you can't say that you haven't been warned."

JT breathes in deeply, smiles, and says, "Okay, but I have one more request."

Both Jen and Kay roll their eyes in consternation and lean in to listen to JT's request.

"All of this must be on the 'down low' until after the tryouts. Okay?"

"Okay by me," Jen answers, shaking her head.

"Yeah, yeah. You told me that before," Kay says. She then turns to Jen as she and JT get up to leave. "Thanks a lot for your time and especially for your advice."

Then, Kay, with a smug smile of which JT ignores, shakes Jen's hand, and says, "We'll probably be seeing you sooner than you think!"

JT stays very close to this regimen. Kay, at first, tries to ignore JT's efforts. But, as time goes on, she is seen at a local elementary school track timing her husband's sprints. She also offers him bottles of water as he needs them.

During one work out, JT agonizes, "These damned wind sprints are killing me, Kay. Besides, the times are way too slow."

"Well, why do you run them so long? Forty yards seems like a long distance to me!" Kay answers.

Rolling his eyes, JT explains, "That's the distance that they test—especially for running backs. If you don't get below five seconds, they won't even look at you."

Kay innocently asks. "Well, if you don't mind my suggesting, why don't you try running uphill so your muscles can build up some more?" Pointing, Kay continues. "How about that nice incline over there on the other side of the track, you know, where the kids go sleigh riding in the winter?"

Slightly dumbfounded, JT scratches his head, nods, and replies, "Okay, that sounds pretty good to me. Thanks, Hon, I think I'll try that. I've got a few more weeks to go."

A couple weeks go by, and JT is seen charging down the same elementary school track. He finishes, then whoops in jubilance when Kay relates the time.

CHAPTER 7

It's Thursday evening, JT can't finish dinner, and he nervously gets ready to go to the stadium to meet the coach, get his gear, and the schedule for the try-outs. Watching him putting on his hooded sweats, and adjusting the hood, Kay good-naturedly jests, "Oh, going incognito, I see!"

"I just want to make it through the tryouts. I'm just going to grab my stuff and I'll be right back," JT replies.

JT enters the stadium and makes his way outside the locker room where there is a small line of prospective players feeding into a table with position coaches, meeting each one, and shaking hands. Then, they are directed to another line of tables where they are given their schedules and equipment. JT breathes a sigh of relief as he notices that he is not the only one wearing a hooded sweatshirt.

He reaches the table, and after JT is asked what position, he is directed to Coach Stanton. As JT approaches, Stanton extends his hand as JT says, "JT Tichi, you called."

"That's right. Congrats at this juncture, but believe me, this is only the beginning. Will you be ready to rock on Saturday?" Stanton snorts with a smile.

"I'm ready right now, Coach!" JT answers.

"A little warning—we'll be starting with the wind sprints." Stanton infers.

"Good, I'm below five in the forty."

"Excellent. I'm sure everyone else is down around there too! You know Shaun Rahmon from the Packers, and Tony Elkins from the Jets?" asks Stanton.

JT nods as Stanton continues. "Well, they were released from their respective pro contracts, and they both decided that they want to give the Dogs a whirl."

Being careful not to show his surprise, JT confidently smiles and replies, "I'll be ready more than ever, Coach. Thanks for the warning."

"Good!" says Stanton and points to the tables behind him. "Pick up your schedule and light equipment—shorts, helmet, tee shirt, and cleats. You have to supply your own jock. After the first cut, you'll get your pads and a locker."

JT nods, shakes Stanton's hand, and as he steps toward the tables, Stanton barks, "Good luck, son!"

JT looks down, hiding a huge grin.

When JT arrives home, he eagerly dons his newly issued tee shirt and Bull Dogs helmet in front of Kay and smugly asks, "Well, Ding, how do I look?"

"Not too shabby for an old dork!" Kay sarcastically replies. Then she giggles and points at JT's helmet. "That bulldog on your helmet is an uncanny resemblance of you!"

"Well, you'll never know what he said, Kay!" JT says excitedly.

"Okay! Okay! What'd he say? What'd he say? I can't stand the suspense!" Kay continues, trying to control her laughter.

"He said, and I quote, 'Good luck, son!'" JT replies, emphasizing the "son" part.

"Oh Lord! Save me!" Looking upward and clasping her hands, Kay swoons. "Will I ever live through this ordeal?"

After JT continues to strut around in his Omaha Bulldogs helmet and tee shirt for quite some time, he takes his helmet off, and Kay approaches. "Honey, will fans be allowed to watch the tryouts? I would just love to be there and support…"

JT interrupts. "Um, oh, sweetheart, I know that you'd love to be there, but there's something about this that I would just feel better doing this alone, by myself. You know that I appreciate your support, and please understand that…"

"Okay. Okay, I understand. Just know that my heart will be with you every step of the way." Kay ends with a smile.

CHAPTER 8

It's Saturday morning, and JT is the first to arrive in the Bulldog locker room. As others slowly arrive, he changes into his shorts, tee shirt, cleats, and helmet. He checks the schedule on the bulletin board then heads out onto the field and begins to loosen up.

Other players follow and do the same. Soon, head coach Chuck Bronte enters the field, followed by several of the offensive and defensive position coaches, who station themselves at different locations on the field. Then, there's a shrill blast of a whistle. At the same time, Coach Bronte is in the middle of the field signaling the players to gather toward him. The assistant coaches encourage the players to gather close to the head coach.

Most players are removing their helmets. JT and a few others keep theirs on. After all of the players are together, Coach Bronte delivers his congratulatory welcoming speech with encouragement, and the fact that there will be just one cut after the basic workouts, then one more after the regular scrimmaging with pads. After that cut, the final Omaha Bulldog roster will be announced. Coach Bronte reminds his players that this is all written in their schedules, and if there are any questions, they should contact their position coaches. With that, he raises his voice and says, "When you hear the whistle, report to your coach." He then points and calls out each position, and the coach's name.

Coach Bronte shouts. "Good Luck!" With a blast of his whistle, the players disperse.

JT is the first to arrive where Coach Stanton is waiting. As the others arrive, he recognizes the ex-Jet, Tony Elkins. JT counts eleven prospective running backs as Stanton begins. "First, we'll do some simple calisthenics, then agility sprints, and we'll finish with timed wind sprints. I needn't remind you that you should hydrate yourselves whenever you need it." He then gestures toward two men with whistles around their necks and holding clip boards, and says, "This is Bill and Tom, my assistants. If there aren't any questions, let's get your helmets back on, form a circle around these guys, and they'll lead you through some exercises."

Elkins lines up alongside JT and mumbles several expletives as the players go through the calisthenics.

After the last stretching exercise, they begin the agility drills. This exercise is especially designed for running backs. They consist of changing position every five and ten yards while carrying a football. Coach Stanton observes, making notes on his clipboard.

JT tries to avoid Elkins, who seems to be continuously, nonstop with his expletives. Finally, one player pleads, "Hey Elkins can you just cut the crap?"

"Oh, go screw yourself, retard!" Elkins retorts.

JT slides between the two as they glare at each other and step toward each other. Stanton blows his whistle and shouts, "Okay! Okay! Break it up over there! Now, let's take a break and get ready for the wind sprints."

The players move around and gravitate toward the table on the sidelines where the water bottles are.

After about ten minutes, Stanton moves to the goal line and says, "We'll just run a couple sprints to loosen up, then we'll time a couple. We know who you are by the number on your tee shirts, and keep those helmets on."

JT and three others move to the goal line where one assistant is stationed with his stopwatch and clipboard. The other assistant trots down to the forty-yard line and waves. As JT gets down into his three-point stance, the others follow. The assistant on the goal line, in a low voice says, "Ready." Then, with a sharp shrill of the whistle, JT and the three others are off and running. All four seem to finish at about the same time. They slow down after fifteen more yards and turn around, swinging their arms, bending down, and breathing deeply. The remaining seven follow. Elkins continues to mutter as he finishes first in this group. JT notices one other player quite a bit behind.

The sprints are repeated from the forty-yard line to the goal line and back again, with short breaks in between. JT learns that his best time was 4.8 seconds and is quite pleased. He knows that he isn't the fastest nor is he the slowest.

Finally, Coach Stanton shouts, "Okay guys! Good work out! Go in and shower, and I'll see you here at six, Monday night."

As the players file into the locker room, JT over-hears one complaining about Elkins's incessant com-

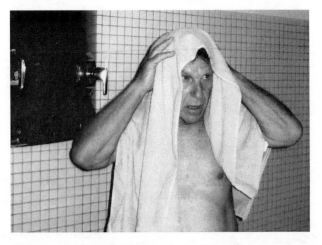

plaints and says, "Just ignore him. You can understand that's obviously one of the reasons the Jets let him go."

"Yeah, I guess you're right. It sure makes sense. Hey! You sure looked good out there today!" the player replied.

"Thanks! You did too!" JT said with a smile.

JT quickly gets to his locker, strips down, throws a towel over his head, and heads for the shower. There, he quickly showers, steps out, and puts the towel over his head again. He returns to his locker, quickly dries off, and slips his sweatshirt on, flips the hood over his head, and heads out the door. He follows this procedure for the rest of the tryouts.

It's late in the afternoon when JT arrives home. After getting out of his car, he starts taking out the lawn mower, when Kay pulls into the driveway and jumps out of her car, shouting, "How was it? How was it?"

"It was okay, a bit grueling, but okay." JT answers. "The wind sprints were killers. I wasn't the fastest, but I wasn't the slowest either!"

Realizing that JT is about to cut the lawn, Kay lurches toward him and offers, "Here! Here! Let me help. I can do that!"

"Oh! Wow, Ding! Now, where the heck have you been all spring?" JT asks with a smile.

"You dork! I'm just trying to help!" Kay smiles back.

They hug. "Let me get this, then we can go out for dinner, and we'll talk about it some more. I need a little down time, anyway." JT suggests.

"Okie dokie!" Kay answers, as JT returns to the lawn mower.

CHAPTER 9

The light workouts continue for a few more practice sessions. In Kay's words, JT manages to remain as "incognito as possible." The running backs' numbers have fallen to eight. The other positions have slightly fallen as well.

About a week later, Coach Stanton announces that it is time to don the pads, and get ready for the real business. He then has his assistants distribute the position playbooks, along with the practice uniforms and pads.

"We'll have a couple skull sessions with the playbooks, before we go full contact. Check the times in the new schedule." Stanton orders.

Remaining as incognito as he can, JT attends the two "skull" sessions, which are with the whole offensive team. They turn out to be a bit uneventful, but quite informative for JT, since his years away from the

game. Finally, the first day of contact arrives, and as usual, JT is dressed out in his pads, with a towel over his head, sitting by his locker, going over his playbook.

Tony Elkins, who has just finished dressing, sidles up to JT, and says, "Yo, punk, if you don't know those plays by now, you'll never know them!"

JT slowly glances up at him and asks hesitantly, "Did you say, 'Punk,' son?"

Each slowly rise from their sitting positions. JT's towel slides off his head, exposing his gray sideburns. He glares nose to nose at Elkins.

"Whoa! Whoa there old man! I really didn't mean…" Elkins stammers.

Before Elkins can finish, JT interjects, "Well, what is it, boy? Punk? Or will it be old man? Let's just see out on the field, boy."

With that said, JT turns and makes his way out onto the playing field on one side of the fifty-yard line and begins loosening up. Other players on the offense begin filing out and line up for calisthenics. On the other side of the field, the defense does the same.

During the warm-ups, a few light and funny barbs are shouted across the field. Coach Stanton walks up and down the lines of players reminding them that he will call the player's numbers before a set of plays, and each player should be prepared to play until he is replaced.

"Be prepared to play four to five plays in each set. We will have periodic breaks, and start all over again until I've seen enough for today."

He then points to three men dressed in white shorts and sweatshirts behind the sidelines and shouts. "These are your trainers. Check in with them, especially if you think you have an injury. And don't forget to stay hydrated."

Finally, two referees arrive, a whistle is blown, and the scrimmage begins.

JT is standing on the sideline, waiting for his number, nineteen, to be called. After the first two sets of plays and a short break, Coach Stanton yells, "Nineteen!"

Before JT runs onto the field, Stanton says, "Go in at the two slot. Let's see what you can do."

JT enters the huddle, and the quarterback calls for a pass play. This particular play has the quarterback faking a hand off to the "two back," JT, before he throws the pass. The ball is snapped. JT takes the fake, but the ball falls incomplete. The next play is another pass, which calls for JT to block on the right side. This time the pass is complete.

The next play calls for the "two back" to actually take the hand off and run through the line, just past the offensive tackle, and the quarterback fakes the pass. When the huddle breaks, JT takes a deep breath, as he lines up for the play, he listens for the count. The ball is snapped; he takes the ball and heads toward the line. The tackle falls down, and the defensive lineman lunges toward JT. Switching the ball to his right side, he stiff-arms the defensive lineman and shoots into the defensive secondary. He sidesteps a diving linebacker, hurdles over the cornerback, and keeps on running for the goal line. The players on the sideline begin to cheer. The whistle blows, but JT keeps on running and doesn't stop until he crosses the goal line.

JT comes back into the huddle after shaking several hands of the offensive players on the way. This quarterback wastes no time with another play. This time it's the same play except on the other side. JT—catching his breath—breaks out of the huddle, assumes his stance, and waits for the count.

This time, JT gets the ball and immediately switches it to his left side, noticing that the defensive lineman has a hand already on his right shoulder. JT spins around, which causes him to break free from the lineman's grasp. He continues toward the sideline, avoiding the linebacker. But the cornerback catches up to him at the sideline. JT spins and sidesteps to his right, losing the defensive back, and heads for the goal line once again. Now it becomes a foot race to the goal line with the safety. JT veers slightly to the left and does not slow down until he crosses the goal line once again. The yells from the offensive sideline are louder this time.

By the time JT gets back to the huddle, he finds another player has replaced him. When he gets back to the sideline, he's congratulated with pats on the back, his butt, and high-fives. As he makes his way over to the training table for some water, he notices Elkins standing by the water cooler. They glance at each other, and without saying a word and keeping his helmet on, JT glares back, and grins widely.

As the scrimmage progresses, JT is called in for more plays. Each time he carries the ball; he displays a unique zigzag technique, with positive gains in yardage, but not quite as prominent as his first two carries of the day. Coach Stanton blows the final whistle and announces that the next scrimmage will be tomorrow at the same time and to be ready. As JT heads for the tunnel that leads to the locker room, he feels a tug on his shoulder and hears Coach Stanton say, "Hey, nineteen, great practice! Keep up the good work!"

"Oh! Um! Yeah! I just got a little lucky today, I guess!" JT managed to blurt out.

"No! Really! You've got some great moves out there, son! Keep it going!" Stanton replies.

"Thanks, coach! See you tomorrow." JT says, again hiding a big smile, as he heads for the locker room.

The next day, JT receives a call from his physician, Dr. Harrington, from the VA. "I just wanted to call and check up on you. How are you doing? Oh! And don't lie to me! I'm your physician, you know!"

"I'm just fine and dandy! We had our first scrimmage, and I'm doing a lot better than I ever thought I would, Jen." JT answers.

"Now, don't lie to me. Do you have any aches or pains?" Jen prods.

"Look, Jen, I appreciate your concern. I feel great! Besides, I promised both you and Kay that if anything happens I would be totally up front with you. I'm feeling just great. There are a couple more scrimmages left. If anything happens, I will keep you informed."

"Well, okay, then. That's right. Just keep me informed. How's Kay taking all of this so far?" Jen asks.

"Oh, she's tolerating all of this, and me, just fine! Actually, Jen, she's been the greatest support for me." JT answers.

"Okay, that's so good to hear. Now, ah…I've got to go. Remember, don't hesitate to call me, you've got my cell number. And the best of luck to you!" Jen replies in closing. JT puts down the receiver and smiles.

Before the evening of the next scrimmage, JT relates his satisfaction of his positive performance of that initial scrimmage to Kay. He also relates what Coach Stanton said to him afterward, which included the coach's reference to him as "son" again!

"Oh, honey! I knew you'd be doing well! But that "son" part is just an old expression!" She says with a laugh.

"Okay! Okay! I know. But it's nice to hear it anyway!" JT replies. "Do you still want to go to a scrimmage? I mean, if you still want to go…"

"Are you kidding me?" Kay screams. "Are you kidding me? You're damned right I want to go! What time and where tomorrow?"

"Okay! Okay! We'll grab a light snack around four tomorrow, then leave for the stadium at about five. I like to get there early, you know." JT suggests.

"Oh boy! Oh boy! Can't wait! Can't wait!" Kay shouts back.

"Now, don't expect anything spectacular. You know both the offense and defense will be toughening up as these scrimmages progress," JT adds.

"Oh, honey! I know you'll do just great, and I want you to know that you'll never, never disappoint me. I love you, you dork!" she says with a grin.

"Thanks, ding." JT replies with a hug.

The following evening, Kay and JT enter the stadium, and JT directs Kay to the stadium seats along the fifty-yard line where other fans and relatives are being seated.

"Okay, sweetie, I'll meet you here after the scrimmage." JT says.

"Okay, honey. Now, good luck! I know you'll give it your best." Kay replies and waves, as JT heads for the locker room.

This scrimmage starts and progresses as the previous one. In one particular running play that JT takes the hand off and dives through the line, he breaks through and is immediately tackled by a charging cornerback. This defensive back winds up, pinning JT to the turf, face guard to face guard.

Looking at each other, and with JT's helmet slightly tipped up, exposing more of his countenance and gray temples, the defensive back blurts out in a raspy whisper, "Holy crap! Doc! Doctor Tichi! What! What the hell are you doing here?"

JT releases the ball and grabs the defensive player's jersey under his chin and harshly whispers, "Brad! It's you! Now Brad, shut up! Please be quiet about this!"

"But! But! How? What the...!" Brad stammers.

At this time the referees run over to the two, who are slowly rising and still sputtering at each other. "Okay! Okay! Break it up! Let's play some ball! Get back to your huddles!"

"Brad! Not a freaking word! You got me?" JT continues. "Oh! Nice tackle!"

JT goes back to his huddle and Brad goes back on defense, still muttering to himself.

The next play is a pass that goes incomplete. JT and Brad still scope out each other.

The following play, another pass is called, but Brad intercepts it. He heads for the sideline and breaks loose for the goal line. At the same time, JT darts toward the sideline and quickly nails Brad with an outstanding tackle of his own. A roar comes from the small crowd and the sidelines.

As JT gets up, he pulls Brad up after him and says, "Remember, not a word, Brad. Not until the last cut."

"Gotcha, Doc! Don't worry. I'll see you after the scrimmage." Brad replies, after getting to his feet with JT's help. "Oh! Nice tackle!"

Once again Coach Stanton congratulates his players and reminds them of the time for the next scrimmage. As usual, JT is the first in the shower and the first to be dressed with his hooded sweatshirt on. Just as he steps toward the door, Brad approaches and whispers, "Doc! Doc Tichi! It's me, Brad! No wonder I haven't recognized you with that hood on!"

With an intensive look, JT replies, "Oh, Brad! Ah, please understand that I need to be as clandestine as possible until the tryouts are over. I just need this chance. I have this need to…"

"It's okay! Doc, it's okay! As a matter of fact, I think it's pretty damned cool!" Brad interjects. "You have my word, Doc. Mum's the word! You can trust me."

"I bet you really want to tell your dad about this!" JT whispers back with a grin.

"Dad? Dad—hell!" Brad bursts out, with a smile and a laugh. "It's my grandpa who I can't wait to tell!"

"Okay!" JT hesitates and laughs. "I'm sure you'll have the chance to spread the news by next week. And thanks for your cooperation, Brad. I really appreciate it." JT graciously replies.

"By the way, where'd you learn how to tackle like that?" Brad asks with a wry smile.

"Oh, back in the Sems. You know, back in the old days. I went both ways. You know, both sides of the ball." JT answers.

"Wow! I'm sure glad you aren't trying out for defensive back. I'd be in real trouble!" Brad retorts with a smile.

"With the way you've been playing, you shouldn't have anything to worry about." JT adds.

"I can say the same for you! Wow! I was just so shocked that number nineteen was you! Wow! I still can't get over it!" Brad says excitedly.

"Well, get over it!" JT says with a smile. "By the way, how's school going for you?"

"Great, Doc. Two more classes and I'll have my associate's in construction management." Brad says proudly.

"Well, keep it up, Brad. You know you can't play football all your life." JT says with a smirk.

"Yeah right, look at you! I think I kind of know what you mean." Brad quips with a smile.

They bump fists and high five as they depart, and JT adds, "The best of luck to you!"

"Thanks, Doc. And the best of luck to you too!" Brad adds.

JT then finds Kay in the stands, chatting with some fans. As soon as she breaks free, she sees the hooded JT, and slowly approaches. They embrace.

She then glistens as she hugs him again and excitedly says, "My goodness! I do have to say that you are doing quite well. And I don't know if I should tell you this or not, but you're obtaining a bit of a crowd base…you know, fans, like in fan club!"

"Oh, I'm just trying to do the best I can." JT shyly reports.

As they walk out of the stadium toward the parking lot, Kay asks, "By the way, I have two questions. One, how are you feeling? Secondly, what was that ruckus with that d-back when he tackled you? I saw that you nailed him back a couple plays later when he intercepted that pass."

"First, I feel just great, and thanks for asking. Secondly, that was my former student, who, at that moment, found out exactly who and what he was tackling. I have to admit, he was a bit surprised!" JT answered with a giggle.

"Oh! Wow! He must have had the shock of his life!" Kay replied.

"Not as much as when I told him to keep his mouth shut about me!" JT shot back with a smile. "Actually, he was pretty cool with it. He said that he understands and will remain quiet about it until the tryouts are over."

"JT! You didn't threaten him! Did you?" Kay sternly asks.

"Well… um…ah… no, not exactly." JT sputters. "Of course not! We actually had a good talk in the locker room afterward, and he was very understanding about the whole thing."

"Okay, you dork. Take me home! I'm tired and I have a sore throat from screaming my lungs out at you!" Kay orders.

"Wow, ding! Now that's a first!" JT quips as they laugh and get into their car and drive home.

CHAPTER 10

As JT predicted, the quality of play as the scrimmages progress increases. For the next three scrimmages, JT's performances remain quite consistent. It's now the evening of the last scheduled scrimmage for the tryouts. There are now six running backs remaining, after two more had left on their own volition. Two more are slated to be cut.

After the last scrimmage, the head coach announces that each player who makes the roster will be called and scheduled to come in and sign their contracts.

"I can tell you right now. Don't figure on bargaining! We're on an extremely tight budget. So, those of you who make it, consider yourselves very lucky! Thanks for your time and good luck to you all! You should know within the next couple of days."

With their recent accolades in the pros, JT reasons to himself that both Shaun Rahmon and Tony

Elkins seem to be sure bets to make the squad. The three other players that he is competing against were recently released from various professional practice teams. Although JT reasons that he has been performing just as well, if not better, than these players, he refuses to become overly confident, even when Kay prods him for his opinion the minute that he steps in through the door.

Then, with her arm around him, Kay quietly says, "Oh, JT, honey, you know that you're going to do alright. I can tell that you're agonizing."

"I'm sorry that I show it, but I think it'll be close, and it would be such a shame to come all this way, and…you know…" JT stammers.

"Look, JT! I know, and you know, that you gave it your best shot! Besides, even if you do make the cut, they're going to, sooner or later, find out about your age, anyway!" Kay interjects.

"You're right. I kind of forgot about that part. You're right, I should be thankful that I got this far… yeah, who would have ever thought?" JT replies, shaking his head with a grin.

Before he sits down, the telephone rings. Kay answers, then hands the receiver over to JT, and says, "Here, Hon, it's for you."

"Who is it? Oh, one of my students? Did they ask for Dr. Tichi?" JT asks.

"No, it's Coach Stanton, now just relax!" replies Kay.

JT grabs the phone and takes a deep breath.

"JT here. Hi, Coach, that was pretty fast, I, I just got through the door."

JT hesitates, then, with each ecstatic "Yes!" his smile becomes wider and wider.

"Okay! No, I don't have to teach on Monday, so tomorrow at three at the Embassy Suites, across from the stadium. Okay! Okay! Ask at the front desk. Okay! I'll be there!"

He puts the receiver down and begins dancing around the living room, only stopping to hug Kay, and shouting, "Yes! Yes! I made it! I made it!"

"Now, honey, just be ready…for, you know… when the truth comes out about your, you know…" Kay stammers.

"Oh, babe! I'm just so happy that I made it! Yes, if they let me play, despite my age, that would certainly be sweeter!" JT relates, with a deep breath and continues. "I promise. I won't be disappoint…well, ah, maybe a little, ah maybe somewhat…"

"Uh oh! Now, heaven for bid! If they decide to sign you, ah…um…won't you need some, or a little legal help, just in case? How about calling Subby, you know, our attorney, who lives just next door? He should, at least, be filled in, so he'll have an idea of what you're trying to do." Kay suggests.

"Great idea, Kay!" JT excitedly replies.

He picks up the phone, dials, and says, "Subby? This is JT. Yeah, well, I want to know if you could help me out. I know you're retired and all that, but I just might be signing a contract soon and I'm wondering…It's a…It's a professional football contract!" JT finally stammers.

"What do you mean you know?" JT asks in total shock. "How the hell did you find out?"

"You what? You went to all those tryouts?" JT asks, with a great deal of astonishment. He glances at Kay, who is shaking her head in disbelief. "Listen, Subby, I'm going to put you on the speaker, so Kay can hear you too."

"Okay, okay. Can you guys hear me?" asks Subby.

"Yeah, go ahead." JT says, putting down the receiver.

"Anyway, I'm actually representing a couple other players, and I thought I should watch these tryouts, so I can have a 'leg up' on what you guys go through. And you know what? As soon as I learned that number nineteen was you, I was actually waiting for this call! What the hell took you so damned long?" Subby asked jokingly.

"But how did you find out that was actually me?" inquired JT.

"Well now, you know how word gets around. Besides, I'm a damned lawyer and I'm sworn to privacy! And you can trust me, JT," Subby sternly answers and continues. "How did you learn how to play like that, and especially at your age?"

"Okay, Subby. Now that's why I need your help and advice. I do want to play. I have a feeling that they—the powers to be: coaches, owners, etc.—won't want to sign me once they learn of my age. I have been disguising it the best way I can so far. Now I've just learned that I made the team, and I've been invited to sign a contract on Monday." JT replies.

"JT, first, I'm going to tell you what I told my other two clients. That is not to have me present. Just gander at the offering, and tell them you'd like to take it to your attorney, and if all is okay, you sign it, make a copy, and deliver the original ASAP." Subby advises and continues, "Secondly, and in your case, be very gracious, up front, and honest. Their main concern will undoubtedly be the health issue. You should know that. But in this day and age, it may not be such an issue. Now, I don't want to build your hopes up, but just be prepared."

"Okay, Sub," JT sternly replies.

"Yes, Sub. Thank you so much." Kay replies.

Sub replies. "And don't forget, let me know immediately what the results are. In the meantime, I will be researching some other similar salaries of that nature. And oh, yes, I would love to represent you!"

"Don't worry, Sub, you'll be the second one to know after Kay! Okay. Bye." JT switches the speaker off and begins his dancing again. This time, his moves seem a bit slower.

"Oh, you're such a dork!" Kay interjects with a hug.

"You know that I could never have made it without you," JT replies with a smile as they embrace again.

CHAPTER 11

Monday arrives, and JT leaves for the Embassy Suites Hotel. He smiles as he recalls Kay's advice right before she left in the morning for her counseling position at the local high school.

Once again she shook her finger at him saying, "Now, no hoodie!" Then, she wished him luck.

JT pulls into the Embassy Suites parking garage. And as per usual, JT is a half hour early for his appointment. He approaches the main desk and inquires. "Um, Coach Bronte? The Bulldogs football team?"

"Yes sir!" replies the young man behind the check in desk. Pointing down the hallway, he continues, "It's Room 315. You may take the elevator or the stairs."

JT thanks him and proceeds to the elevator. The doors open, and JT is met with several news reporters and a TV cameraman. He squeezes in and says, "Could someone push the third floor button?"

A voice from the rear says, "Don't worry, pal! We're all going there!"

The elevator stops at the third floor. As soon as the door slides open, JT is virtually shoved aside as the news people burst their way out and bolt toward Room 315, which is diagonally across a large hallway. There is already a contingent of news media people crowded around one young man who JT quickly recognizes as Tony Elkins. Within a few minutes, the door to Room 315 opens, and out comes Shaun Rahmon, who is immediately engulfed with the media people. Coach Stanton calls Elkins in and the door is immediately closed. JT, in the meantime, recognizes Stu Lerner, the local sportscaster amongst the others crowding around Rahmon.

When Shaun and JT recognize each other, Shaun pathetically holds up his hands. He then points to JT with one hand and to his head with the other with a puzzled look on his face. JT realizes immediately that Shaun is gesturing toward JT's gray hair. JT just shrugs and smiles back. JT turns and slowly retreats into the crowded hall, while Shaun continues to chat with the news people. JT manages to remain inconspicuous by quietly withdrawing to an empty chair, taking in the busyness of this event.

After about fifteen minutes, the door to Room 315 opens, and out comes Elkins. The door closes and Elkins immediately recognizes JT. Two newscasters quickly gravitate toward Elkins. Pointing toward JT, Elkins blurts, "Hey guys! Here's the dude you should be interviewing!" As he gets closer to JT, he spurts, "Congrats, old man! I always knew you could do it!"

Before JT could say anything, the door to Room 315 opens, and Coach Stanton calls, "Joe Tichi! Is Joseph Tichi here yet? You are our last one for today."

A bit perplexed for the moment, JT steps toward Stanton, and answers, "Here, sir! I'm right here!"

"Well, step right in." Eyeballing JT's gray head as JT brushes past. Stanton closes the door and Coach Bronte, also noticing JT's gray head, slowly begins the introductions, "I'd like you to meet some people. Hey, everybody, this is Bulldog running back Joe Tichi."

"Hi! I go by JT. You can call me JT." JT smiles.

Gesturing toward each individual, Bronte haltingly begins. "You should know Coach Stanton."

JT nods and proceeds to shake hands with each person that he meets.

"This is Jack Sims, president of the Bulldogs; the Bulldog's attorney, Mick Davidson, attorney at law from Eaton Rock Law; Fred Rose, part owner; Laura Bund, another part owner; and this guy stuck behind the computer is Phil Dorfer. Phil is Jack's secretary, and you can congratulate him. He just completed his bachelor's degree in Business Management and Information Technology."

After shaking Phil's hand, Phil and JT momentarily look at each other as if they recognize one another. At the same time, Coach Bronte leans over to Coach Stanton, and whispers, "Are you sure this is that same number nineteen? I don't know about you, but he looks a hell of a lot older than I expected!"

"Yeah, you're right. I'll ask him straight up, and I'll have Phil pull his application before we go on any further." Stanton whispers back and immediately confers with Phil.

JT sits and smiles nervously at the owners, the attorney, and the president. They, in turn, reflect the same uncomfortable stares.

While Phil rustles through some papers alongside his laptop, Coach Stanton, without any further adieu asks, "Joe, um…ah, JT…just…ah, how old are you? I don't mean to embarrass you, but…"

"Oh, um…it's okay…I…um…" JT stammers.

Before JT can answer Stanton's question, Phil jumps up, hands Stanton the application, and excitedly blurts out, "I knew it! I knew it! Doctor Tichi! It's you! Doctor Tichi! Oh my God! It is you!"

As everyone glares in astonishment, Phil continues, "This is Doctor Tichi, the best college professor there is! I had him as my public speaking instructor a couple years back at the community college! You were terrific, Doc!"

Embarrassingly, JT nods, smiles, and motions toward Phil, "Okay, Phil, okay. I recognize you now too. We can talk later."

Realizing his interruption, Phil looks down and embarrassingly apologizes for his outburst. "Oops, sorry everybody." With that, he slowly sinks down and retreats behind his laptop.

Clearing his throat, Stanton commences to repeat his query, as he peruses JT's application. "This says that you were born in nineteen...ah that looks like a three... nah, it couldn't be! There must be some type of error here." He leans toward Bronte for his clarification.

After a momentary gaze, Bronte says, "I can't say for certain, but it sure as hell looks like a freaking thirty nine to me! But that can't be right. Because that would make you..." Bronte ponders.

"Seventy!" JT shouts out in a somewhat proud fashion. "Yes! That does say nineteen thirty-nine! And yes, I'm seventy years old!"

There is a long moment of silence. The owners look at each other, not believing what they have just heard.

The Bulldog president, Jack Sims, is still shaking his head in disbelief and breaks the silence. "We can't possibly sign you up to play professional football, Mr., ah, I mean Dr. Tichi. I'm sure you know the reasons, or at least the primary reason why."

He glances at the attorney, Mick Davidson, and both nod in agreement.

The owners are continually whispering to each other. Bronte is still staring at JT in wonderment. Stanton now has his head in his hands mumbling, "Oh my God… Oh my God…"

"Yes," JT replies. Addressing the owners, he continues, "The primary reason would be your concern for my health and well being while participating in this activity." Turning toward Davidson, he continues, "But I'm here before you today to tell you that I'm agreeable to sign any affidavit in my contract that would exonerate this franchise of any health issue that I would incur while playing football for this organization."

There is a long pause. Stanton and Bronte both look longingly at Sims. Sims and Davidson both shake their heads and grimace as they turn to the owners who both have blank looks of wonderment.

JT breaks the silence. "Well, in parting, I would like to thank all of you, especially Coach Bronte and Coach Stanton for this wonderful experience. I completely understand the dilemma that I have caused. But I humbly appreciate your permitting me to help fulfill a lost dream that I always yearned to complete."

He turns toward Phil and motions with his hand to his head, as if on the telephone and says, "Call—we'll talk."

As he walks toward the door, Phil excitedly jumps up from behind his laptop again and pleads, "People! People! Please! I'd like to say something. Please, I think I have a valid suggestion!"

JT stops and turns. All eyes are on Phil. Then, they shift their stares back at Jack Sims, the president of the Bulldogs. "Okay, Phil. What do you have to say? Try to make it quick, we've all had a long day."

Taking a deep breath, Phil begins, "Okay. Now I've been thinking about the basics of the business that we are in." He pauses, and then continues. "We all have to agree that it's entertainment. Yes, entertainment."

Sims rolls his eyes as Phil plods on. "Now, what does the entertainment business thrive on? Where does it obtain its revenue?" After a quick pause, Phil answers. "Tickets! And also advertising!"

"Oh, brother! Where is this kid going with this?" Sims mumbles, glancing up at his attorney, who, to Sims' astonishment, is actually paying attention.

"Yes, that's right! Tickets and advertising! Now, let's take each one and apply them to Dr....err...ah... JT's situation. Think about it! Now, who would actually want to see...um, JT play football?" Phil pauses. "Sure I would, and I'm sure all of you would too. But let's step back and view it from a broader spectrum."

The largest growing segment of the population in our society happens to be the baby boomers. The older citizens, especially those who are sixty and older, and as I perceive it, they would love to see a seventy-year-old play some serious football! Wouldn't they?"

The owners nod, and look at each other. Then Laura Bund says to the other owner, Fred Rose, "My dad sure would, Fred. Wouldn't yours?" Fred nods.

"Okay! Now the biggie!" Phil excitedly drives on. "Advertising! Just think of all those health products for the elder…ah…um…seniors in our society! If JT is anywhere near as successful on the field as he has proven already, could you imagine how much support that those companies would offer? Think about it!"

"Oh my goodness!" Laura Bund pipes up. "All those creams for the old age spots, and not to mention those vitamins and supplements!"

"Crap!" blurts Fred. "What about Viagra and, and Cialis and, and…oops!"

A little embarrassed after catching Laura Bund's glances, he shyly glances down and covers his mouth.

JT bursts out in laughter, followed by everybody else in the room. While the laughter begins to subside, Bulldog president, Sims, consults with Mick Davidson, the attorney. Then, taking a few moments to settle down, Sims raises his arms to quiet down the room, signaling that he wants to speak.

When it's quiet enough, he turns to JT. "JT, just what type of medical coverage would you have, say, if we did actually go along with your proposal?"

"Well, I do have medicare!" JT answers with a smile. They all laugh. "But, I also have, who I consider my personal physician, Dr. Jennifer Harrington from the VA. I am a vet. And, by the way, she was informed, and I consulted with her via a thorough physical examination before the tryouts. And I plan to consult with her in the future."

Coach Stanton lets out a huge, "Yes!" Both he and Bronte proceed to do a high five.

"Okay, could you and the coaches just step outside? We just need to consult for a few more minutes." Sims suggests to JT, and the two coaches.

As soon as JT opens the door, flashes of cameras and newscasters mob him, and the coaches, with microphones and television cameramen. They quickly retreat back into the room. Sims, Phil, and the owners show a bit of surprise after witnessing the commotion.

"Holy cow! You don't suppose word got out already? How'd the hell did that happen? Okay! There is a rear exit that goes to the service elevator over there."

Sims gestures toward a door across the other side of the room and forces a slightly nervous smile. "Could you guys step out there for just a few minutes? I think that's all the time we'll need!"

JT and the coaches oblige and step out the rear door. Once outside, JT says to the coaches, "Did you by any chance notice Elkins in the background?"

"Yeah," Stanton replies, "he was kind of laughing, pointing, and waving!"

"Yeah, I saw him too," says Coach Bronte. "You don't suppose he…"

"Yeah, it wouldn't surprise me if he egged the media on to this. As I recall, he did catch me with my guard down right before the first scrimmage," JT replied.

"Well, that's it!" Coach Stanton says. He turns to Coach Bronte. "You heard me warn him about his attitude not just an hour ago! When is he going to learn?"

"I'll personally warn him myself this time. It'll be the last one for sure!" Bronte answers. "Coach Dickey, from the Jets, warned me about this dude. Damned if he wasn't right!"

Some moments later, the door opens, and Sims motions them back in. As soon as JT and the coaches sit down, Phil approaches and hands JT his contract, and then says, "I've been asked by and on behalf of the Omaha Bulldog Professional Football franchise, and I am so honored, to present this offer to you."

JT stands up and takes the contract. At the same time he shakes Phil's hand, smiles, and whispers, "Thanks for everything, Phil."

JT returns to his seat, peruses the papers for several minutes. He finally looks up and asks, "What about this clause with the National Football League?

I can tell you that I would not be interested in the National Football League, especially if I'm comfortable playing here. Let's face it, and to be honest, there won't be that many annual contracts for me, especially at my age."

"Whew! JT, that was well said. But, what will happen if they do approach you with an offer?" Sims asks.

"I would kindly turn them down. I just think that it would be much too uncomfortable for someone who would be more than happy playing at this level," JT replies. "Besides, and I honestly believe this, money isn't everything!"

Sims and the owners look at each other. They nod, and Sims says, "Okay, but I'll surely leave that open until the time comes, JT. I do, humbly, respect your honesty."

"All I'll need is you and your coaches' support in this matter." JT replies, looking sternly into Sims' eyes.

"Done." Sims replies with an affirming nod.

JT smiles and replies, "Then I believe everything's in order. I particularly like the health package. After my attorney reviews it, and I'm quite sure he will be in favor of it, I will sign, make a copy for myself, then forward the original to you as soon as possible."

A round of congratulatory handshakes and positive murmurs immediately circulate the room.

Raising and waving his hand for the room to be quiet one more time, JT speaks again. "I would just like one request." The room becomes silent, as JT continues. "If there isn't a problem, I would like to wear the number, thirty-nine."

Both Coach Stanton and Coach Bronte glance at each other, a little confused. They whisper, shrug their shoulders, and nod. Coach Bronte, with a somewhat perplexed look on his face says, "Sure, JT. We won't have a problem with that. But, just for curiosity's sake, why that number, thirty-nine?"

Nodding with a wide grin, JT answers. "Well, the primary reason is that was the year I was born." The room breaks out in light laughter as JT pauses, and then continues. "Secondly, if you can remember the great comedian, Jack Benny, in his later years, he became quite annoyed when people asked him his age. So, anytime he was asked, he always said, 'Thirty-nine!'" With that, the room explodes into uncontrolled laughter.

As soon as the jubilance calms down, Sims, the president of the Bulldogs, says to JT, "By the way, just as a reminder, as a result of this media frenzy, if you feel the need for any additional help to wade through it or any other interference, just let us know. If you haven't noticed, I had Phil add that, and other contractual benefits, on the last couple of pages for you."

Addressing everyone in the room, JT rises and begins to speak, teary eyed, and with a smile, "As I said not that long ago, I thank you all for your time and patience."

Everyone smiles as JT continues and turns to the coaches. "In addition, I'm looking forward to a successful season. Thank you."

Sims quickly steps forward and suggests with a wry smile, "At this point, I think we should get the heck out of here! I hope the signings go much quieter tomorrow!"

With that said, they all laugh and gravitate toward the rear door, exiting into the elevator.

JT reaches the parking lot and quickly gets into his car, leaves the parking garage, and heads for home.

As soon as JT walks through his front door, Kay is right there, desperately waiting with her arms crossed. "Well?"

JT grabs her, hugs her, gives her a big kiss, and excitedly says with a big smile, "Here, you can read it yourself!"

Before examining the contract, Kay immediately says, "Oh my goodness! Um... how about calling Subby?"

"I'm on it!" JT excitedly replies.

He picks up the phone, dials, and says, "Subby? JT. Yeah, well, I just got back, and I have it here. Why don't you come over?" JT hangs up the phone and turns to Kay.

She looks up and exclaims, "Wow! All this to just play football?"

"Look at the health clause! Look at the health clause!" JT answers.

At the same time, there's a ring at the front door, and in comes Subby.

Without any hesitation, Kay hands the contract over to Subby. He sits down, puts on his glasses, and quietly reads. JT and Kay watch anxiously.

"Ah huh! Good! Ah huh! Not bad! Oh, very good! Oh, excellent!" Subby happily mutters.

"Okay! Okay! So…is it okay? Should I sign?" JT anxiously asks.

"It's great so far! Now just let me finish." Subby advises, and he proceeds to finish examining the contract.

He finally takes his glasses off, looks at JT, and says, "JT, this is a fine contract. The health issue is covered very nicely. There is even a stipulation for your freedom to work any additional deals for any, and I quote, 'legitimate business or organization that you would give your name in sponsorship of their products.' It's just a great contract for you, JT. And it's a year-to-year deal, of which you would have to agree."

"Okay then. I guess they have a running back! I'll sign it, copy it on my printer, and personally deliver it!" JT says, glancing and smiling at Kay.

"Don't forget to make a copy for my records too," Subby suggests as JT smiles and hugs Subby.

Kay then goes to JT and hugs him. Subby leaves for the door, waves, and says, "I see you two have some celebrating to do."

CHAPTER 12

JT finds that his first season is one of several primary adjustments. First and foremost was his life on the football team. The other adjustments consisted of his life with his fans, and, of course, the changes to his personal life at home. All of these so-called adjustments are perpetuated by the incessant need of the public's right to know, or better known, as the news media.

Right before the start of that first season, Coach Stanton and Coach Bronte informed JT that they planned on easing JT into the lineup. In other words, they would conference with JT before each game as to how much playing time JT wanted to actually play.

By the opening kick-off of the first game, and as a result of the media exposure, fans were more than anxious to see JT play. A considerable amount of booing followed the Bulldogs' first series of offensive plays without their seeing JT in the backfield. When the Dogs got the ball back, Stanton gave JT the nod. The crowd roared as JT ran onto the field.

As a result, JT did not let his fans down. He made several substantial running gains after taking fakes, then a hand off through the line or an around-end running play. JT capped off his first series as a professional running back with a completed pass in the flat and a Bulldog touchdown!

JT played much of that game, only to take a break in the last quarter, with the Bulldogs well ahead by three touchdowns and heading for their first win. This sets the stage of what turns out to be an extremely successful season. After that first game, in the jubilant Bulldog locker room, JT is finishing dressing. He becomes a bit astonished when Tony Elkins approaches.

"Yo, man!" Elkins gestures toward JT for a handshake. "Great game!"

"Thanks, Tony. You played well yourself," replied JT, shaking Tony's hand.

"Um, ah, listen. I…ah…I just want to apologize for any and all that crap I gave you. I really didn't mean any harm. I just talk without thinking sometimes, and…" Tony stammers.

"It's okay, Tony. Now that you realize it was crap," JT replies with a smile. "Let's just take it one game at a time. And let up on the other guys too."

"Thanks, man." Tony nods with a serious look. "I sure will. I'll see you tomorrow. Thanks again."

After Tony leaves, Brad peers around the other side of the lockers and says, "Oh my God! Oh my God!" Brad rails with astonishment. "Did I just hear what I just heard? Was that the same jerk we all know? Was that Elkins? Really?"

JT nods as they both watch Elkins exit the locker room door. Grinning, he continues, "Yep! I'm pretty sure it was him! I was a bit taken aback myself! Just wait until the coaches hear about this!"

Brad continues to shake his head in amazement.

"Hey! Great game today!" JT slaps Brad on the back, changing the subject. "You had some good tackles and you covered those receivers pretty well, Brad."

"J…um Doc, um. Dang! I just can't call you JT for some reason!" Brad stammers. "Doc! You had a great game yourself!"

"Oh Brad! You can call me anything you want!" JT laughs. "Just don't call me late—like late for breakfast, or late for lunch, or late for supper!"

They both laugh, and together they head out the door. As they move toward the parking lot, JT and Brad notice a crowd of fans in the distance. JT says, "Okay, Brad, the young ones are yours and the little old ones are mine!"

"Yikes!" Brad blurts, as they head toward the fans. "I never knew it would be like this!"

CHAPTER 13

As a precursor for the balance of the season, as per usual, at designated areas, barriers are installed to hold the fans back. There is always a designated area for the autograph seekers, the news reporters, radio announcers, and telecasters. There is always a designated detour for the Bulldog players and coaches to get to their cars and to be directed to an escape route out of the stadium parking lot.

These autograph seekers and media people are present both before and after the games. This becomes protocol, especially at the home games. With the Bulldogs' growing success, and, of course, with the help of the media, the fan base broadens. By the end of the season, the numbers increase. This becomes even more prominent at the away games.

Fan appreciation for JT becomes prevalent, especially for the over-the-age-of-fifty category. By the third home game, a cheer group of about twenty is organized by a group of ladies who call themselves "The Gray Bulldog Cheer Squad." A couple of their rules are that you have to be over fifty and physically fit. Most are ladies, but a few men show up too. They also wear white tennis shoes, black slacks, and gray sweaters. The Omaha Bulldog is emblazoned on the front and a red number thirty-nine on the left shoulder. All of this is topped off with red, gray, and white ribbons in the women's hair.

The Omaha Herald will run a feature article in their sports section about this hearty group. After a number of interviews with several cheer squad members, the paper concluded that this organization is one of the best things to happen to this age group in the city of Omaha.

One elderly "JT fan" was quoted. "Not only has it given us something to do, but it's a great source of aerobic exercise."

JT receives continual attention, not only in the local newspaper, but he is also interviewed, and featured, in several national sports magazines. This increases JT's fan base enormously.

The local television sports commentators periodically feature members of the Gray Cheer Squad on their sports programs. JT and Kay are invited to appear on several television talk shows. On one particular health fitness show in Los Angeles, its theme

for the day was *Fitness Techniques for Senior Citizens*. The host is a licensed physical fitness physician, Doctor Dave Gurnsey. JT is asked to demonstrate how he loosens up in preparation for a game.

Decked out in sweats, JT, as requested, shows a step-by-step set of calisthenics he personally uses before each game.

After completing the set, Dr. Gurnsey asks, "Do you do anything special, say, if you get a tightened muscle, or a sore joint, after a bone-jarring tackle?"

"First of all," JT replies, "I am in close contact with my family physician, Dr. Jennifer Harrington, even before I decided to play professional football for the Omaha Bulldogs a couple years ago."

"She actually gave you the 'green light' to play?" Gurnsey interjects.

"No, not really," JT answers with a smile. "You could have called it a 'yellow light!'"

They both laugh as JT continues. "She cautioned me and made me fully aware of the possible ramifications of the results of any injuries for a person of my age, and subsequently, left the decision to play entirely up to me."

"Since playing, and playing quite regularly, have you been given any additional advice, or good health tips?" Gurnsey asks.

"I've been instructed to report immediately to my trainers if I experience any type of soreness, especially after a good hit," replies JT. "The key word here is *immediately*, Doctor Gurnsey. Then, after the trainer examines the area and determines that there is no major break or tear, he will immediately begin massaging the effected area, in order for me to be able to continue playing."

"I'm assuming that this procedure is designed especially for the more senior athlete, such as you?" Gurnsey asks.

"Actually, this procedure should be followed by any athlete, regardless of age." JT answers. "But sure, it's extremely beneficial for an old codger like me!"

"I guess the younger athletes—and I'm sure we did the same thing when we were young–ignore the injury, so we can get back in to play as soon as possible!" Gurnsey adds with a grin.

"On that note, I'm happy to report that all of the players on the Bulldog team are adhering more and more to our trainers' injury procedure, and reporting them as soon as they occur," JT added.

CHAPTER 14

After a visit to New York to appear on a television talk show, JT and Kay dine at an exclusive restaurant. Kay leans over to JT, grins, and says, "Wow! I am sure glad I talked you into trying out for that danged team!"

"Yeah, right! It was all you, baby!" JT replies with a laugh.

They raise their wine glasses, and JT makes a toast. "To our life of happiness. You know I couldn't do all this without you!"

"Oh honey, you're going to make me cry," Kay happily replies as they tip their glasses.

When the news media becomes "relentlessly annoying," in JT's words, he contacts the Bulldog main office. He immediately receives excellent support and relief. Security guards are sent to his home. At first, Kay really didn't mind too much. But before long, she has a change of mind and refers to them as "the damned paparazzi!"

What about JT's home life? Well, during that first season with the Bulldogs, Kay was initially thrilled with all the attention, especially at the high school where she taught. Her fellow teachers, as well as many students, asked a great deal of questions. Typical queries would be if she knew him when he played in the seventies, or if she knew that JT was that talented as a football player. Her answers were that she did not know JT back then, but he always talked about the game and his time in the Sems.

"I have to admit, and I told him this. I thought he was bragging just a little at times!" Kay says with a laugh.

The administration and staff at Kay's school became very helpful, especially after the first few games. They soon began filtering the number of phone calls from the media and other inquiring minds about JT.

JT's second season proves to be just as successful and satisfying as his first. But the high light of this season happens at a game in early November against the Denver Coyotes, at Denver. The football world is still talking about it, and not only the play, but also the proceding interview by the Denver sports telecaster Mike Jayne. It is viewed on tape from time to time.

On the first Bulldog offensive play, JT took a hand off at the line of scrimmage and ran seventy-two yards for a touchdown! When interviewed at the end of the game, of which they won, of course, Jayne asks JT the typical question of how he did it.

Without hesitation and with a wide grin, JT answers, "Well, tomorrow is my birthday, and I just wanted to start celebrating!"

"Oh, ah, happy birthday, JT! But going seventy-two yards for a touchdown on the opening play, you certainly did celebrate, JT! Going back to my question. How did you do it?" Jayne shouts with a forced smile.

JT answers, emphasizing the yardage loudly and smiling. "Yes indeed! *Seventy-two*! I don't think the question is not so much how, but why? Why *seventy-two*?"

After an awkward hesitation, Jayne forms a blank look of astonishment on his face, and then closes his eyes, hitting his hand on his forehead, quickly recovering with, "Oh, like, duh! And a happy seventy-second birthday to you!" They both bust out laughing to end the interview.

Another conference championship and more endorsements follow. Kay and JT soon find it necessary to engage the services of a local financial adviser, who becomes an immediate invaluable aid with JT's sudden increase in wealth. A great deal came from what was predicted, his promotional endorsements.

By the end of that second season, Kay and JT invest in a condo in downtown Omaha. It proves to be an appropriate escape from their home, west of the city, which, at times, fails to afford the privacy that they need. When in the off-season and not involved in commercial advertising or endorsements, believe it or not, JT continues to teach at the community college. His teaching schedule is restricted to the winter quarter and just evening classes in the spring quarter.

Kay decides to retire from her teaching at the high school, and devote more time to traveling and JT's busy schedule.

CHAPTER 15

Let's return to where this story began. The Bulldogs have just celebrated another conference championship. Amongst the recent news about various players, Brad, the defensive back and a former student of JT, has begun negotiating a contract with the Chicago Bears. Both running backs, Tony Elkins and Shaun, have agreed and accepted contracts to play in the Canadian Football League next season. JT, as he originally planned, remains happy, and intends to stay with the Omaha Bulldogs as long as he is able.

Kay and JT are standing on the balcony of their condo in downtown Omaha. It's late in the evening, and they are taking in the beautiful vista before them. The maze of the city lights blends in with the misty, bright, shining stars in the eastern sky.

"Oh, JT," Kay begins, "isn't this just so wonderful?"

"Yeah, honey. Everything is just beautiful." JT replies. He turns to her and continues. "Yes, you and our life together. I couldn't ask for anything more."

"Oh, JT. You're going to make me cry again," Kay whispers.

"Sweetheart, you know I could not do any of this without you," JT whispers back as they embrace.

JT does realize, and Kay reminds him now and then, that he will have to stop playing…some day.

After a long moment of romantic silence, JT points and says, "Hey, babe! What's that gorgeous, winding bridge over there?"

"Oh, that's the Bob Kerrey Bridge. You know, the former governor, medal of honor winner, currently the president of the New School in New York," Kay replies.

"Oh yeah! Hey! Did I ever tell you about the first time I met him? It was back in the sixties, in Quantico, when I was…" JT's voice trails off.

And that's another story.